To Caroline Royds
with thanks

First published 1994 by
Walker Books Ltd, 87 Vauxhall Walk
London SE11 5HJ

This edition published 1998

4 6 8 10 9 7 5

Printed in Hong Kong

British Library Cataloguing in Publication Data:
a catalogue record for this book is
available from the British Library

ISBN 0-7445-6324-0

Jez Alborough

“Dad, there’s something
at the letter box.
What can it be?”

“Be brave, Billy boy, have a look and see.”

“Dad, it’s a **crocodile**!
What shall I do?”

“Ask it in, Billy boy, it can play with you.”

"Dad, there's something at the keyhole. What can it be?"

"Be brave, Billy boy, have a look and see."

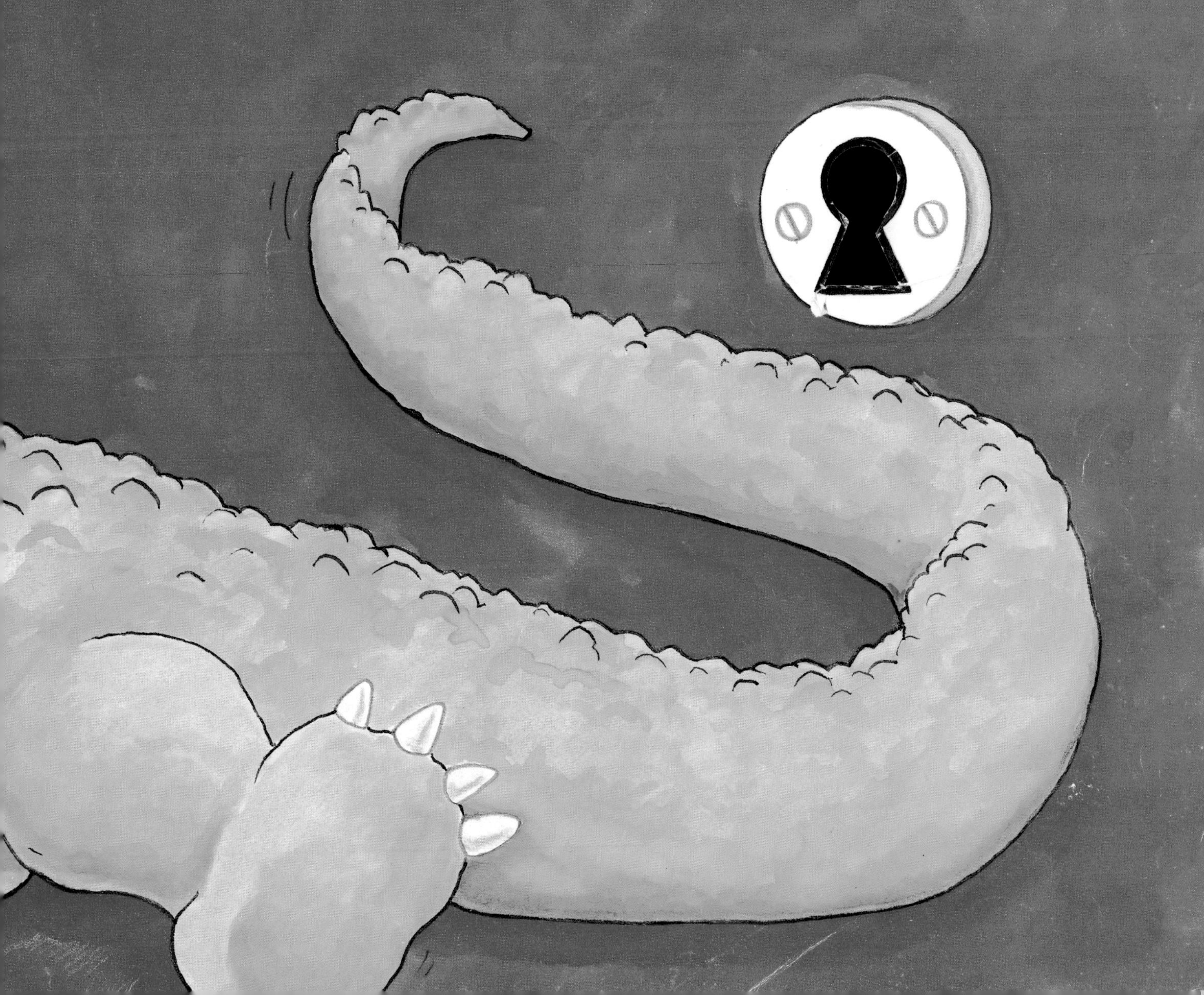

"Dad, it's a **tiger**! What shall I do?"

"Ask it in, Billy boy, it can play with you."

"Dad, there's something
at the window.
What can it be?"

“Be brave, Billy boy, have a look and see.”

"Dad, it's a **bear**!
What shall I do?"

"Ask it in, Billy boy,
it can play with you."

“Dad, there’s something
in the kitchen.
What can it be?”

"Don't be silly,
Billy boy, it's only…"

Me!